POLICE
OFFICERS

by Meg Gaertner

Cody Koala

An Imprint of Pop!

popbooksonline.com

abdopublishing.com

Published by Pop!, a division of ABDO, PO Box 398166, Minneapolis, Minnesota 55439. Copyright © 2019 by POP, LLC. International copyrights reserved in all countries. No part of this book may be reproduced in any form without written permission from the publisher. Pop!™ is a trademark and logo of POP, LLC.

Printed in the United States of America, North Mankato, Minnesota

042018
092018

THIS BOOK CONTAINS RECYCLED MATERIALS

Cover Photo: iStockphoto
Interior Photos: iStockphoto, 1, 6, 9 (top), 9 (bottom left), 9 (bottom right), 12, 16, 19 (bottom); Eddie Quinones/The Times/AP Images, 5; Shutterstock Images, 11, 15, 19 (top left), 19 (top right), 21 (top), 21 (bottom left); M. Spencer Green/AP Images, 21 (bottom right)

Editor: Charly Haley
Series Designer: Laura Mitchell

Library of Congress Control Number: 2017963077

Publisher's Cataloging-in-Publication Data

Names: Gaertner, Meg, author.
Title: Police officers / by Meg Gaertner.
Description: Minneapolis, Minnesota : Pop!, 2019. | Series: Community workers | Includes online resources and index.
Identifiers: ISBN 9781532160141 (lib.bdg.) | ISBN 9781532161261 (ebook) |
Subjects: LCSH: Police--Juvenile literature. | Community policing--Juvenile literature. | Village communities--Law and legislation--Juvenile literature. | Occupations--Careers--Jobs--Juvenile literature. | Community life--Juvenile literature.
Classification: DDC 363.2--dc23

Hello! My name is

Cody Koala

Pop open this book and you'll find QR codes like this one, loaded with information, so you can learn even more!

Scan this code* and others like it while you read, or visit the website below to make this book pop.

popbooksonline.com/police-officers

*Scanning QR codes requires a web-enabled smart device with a QR code reader app and a camera.

Table of Contents

A Day in the Life

Police officers **patrol** an area. They watch for signs that laws are being broken. They also watch for people who might need help.

Watch a video here!

The officers respond to calls about car crashes, crimes, and other emergencies.

The Work

Police officers protect people. They **arrest** people who break the law. They give tickets to unsafe drivers. They keep roads and communities safe.

Learn more here!

People can call 9-1-1 to get help during emergencies. A **dispatcher** answers the call. The dispatcher sends the nearest police officer to help.

Police stations also have a non-emergency number. Sometimes people who feel unsafe or afraid call this number. A police officer can help those people feel safe.

People can ask the police to check on loved ones who they are worried about.

Chapter 3

Tools for Police Officers

Police drive cars with special red and blue lights on top. The lights flash during an emergency. Police also have a loud **siren** for emergencies.

Learn more here!

Police officers use radios
to talk to dispatchers and
other officers. They use

special **codes** so they can speak quickly. Officers have small notebooks so they can take notes while talking to people.

> The code "10-4" means "OK." It means the officer got the message.

Police officers use **handcuffs** to arrest people. Handcuffs go around the wrists of a **suspect**. They make sure the suspect cannot get away.

handcuffs

small notebook

police car with lights

gun

badge

police tape

police radio

Chapter 4

Helping the Community

Police officers also work to stop emergencies before they happen. Officers visit schools and businesses to teach people about safety.

Complete an activity here!

Making Connections

Text-to-Self

Have you ever met a police officer? What did you think? Would you ever want to be a police officer?

Text-to-Text

Have you read other books about community workers? How are their jobs different from a police officer's?

Text-to-World

Why do you think it is important to have police officers? What might the world be like without police officers?

Glossary

arrest – to hold a suspect.

code – special words and numbers used in place of regular words to send messages.

dispatcher – a person who answers 9-1-1 calls.

handcuffs – metal rings that hold a suspect's wrists together.

patrol – to watch an area to keep it safe.

siren – a loud sound that emergency vehicles can use when they need people to get out of their way.

suspect – someone who is believed to have broken the law.

Index

crimes, /

dispatchers, 10, 16

emergencies, 7, 10, 14, 20

helping, 4, 10–13

laws, 4, 8

patrol, 4

radios, 16

safety, 8, 13, 20

Online Resources

popbooksonline.com

Thanks for reading this Cody Koala book!

Scan this code* and others like it in this book, or visit the website below to make this book pop!

popbooksonline.com/police-officers

*Scanning QR codes requires a web-enabled smart device with a QR code reader app and a camera.